I would like to dedicate this book to the visionary people
at Cameron Kids for their dedication to creating a better future
by nurturing the minds and hearts of today's children.

—R.N.R.

The illustrator would like to dedicate this book to
the sparkles in her life: Jacob, Mica, and Calder.
She would also like to give thanks to Dr. Remen for sharing her story
and Melissa, Amy, and Nina at Cameron Kids for bringing it all together.

—R.S.

Text copyright © 2022 Rachel Naomi Remen
Illustrations copyright © 2022 Rachell Sumpter

Book design by Melissa Nelson Greenberg

Published in 2022 by CAMERON + COMPANY, a division of ABRAMS.
All rights reserved. No portion of this book may be reproduced,
stored in a retrieval system, or transmitted in any form or by any means, mechanical,
electronic, photocopying, recording, or otherwise, without written permission from the publisher.

Library of Congress Cataloging-in-Publication Data available.
ISBN: 978-1-951836-34-4

Printed in China

10 9 8 7 6 5 4 3 2 1

CAMERON KIDS is an imprint of CAMERON + COMPANY

CAMERON + COMPANY
Petaluma, California
www.cameronbooks.com

THE BIRTHDAY OF THE WORLD

A STORY ABOUT FINDING LIGHT IN EVERYONE AND EVERYTHING

by Dr. Rachel Naomi Remen

illustrated by Rachell Sumpter

cameron kids

When I was very small my grandfather was my favorite person in the world.

He called me by a special name, Neh-shuma-leh, which means Little Beloved Soul. And he knew many many many stories.

When I turned four
he gave me a very old story
called "The Birthday of the World."

It goes like this . . .

In the beginning,
there was only darkness.

And then a great ray of light
ended the darkness,
and the world was born,
the world of a thousand thousand things.

It was filled with light.

Then something unexpected happened,
and the light of the world broke into
millions and millions of sparks of light.

These sparks fell everywhere.
They fell into everyone
and everything.

They fell into all the people—boys, girls, moms and dads, grandmas and grandpas.
They fell into all the animals—dogs and cats and guinea pigs and rabbits.
They fell into all the fish in the ocean and all the birds in the sky.
They fell into all the plants and all the trees, and into all families.

And they are still there today . . .
hidden in everyone and everything.

This is why you were born
and I was born
and everyone was born—

We were all born because we can each find the spark of light
that is hidden in everyone and everything.

We can become its friend.

We can feed it and help it grow bigger
and shine more brightly.

We can help it grow so bright that it becomes
visible once again.

One spark at a time.

But Grandpa, I asked.
If the sparks of light are hidden and we cannot see them,
how can we find them?

Ah! Neh-shuma-leh, said my grandpa.
We can't see them with our eyes.
We can only see them with our hearts.

Only your heart can see the spark of light
that is hidden in everyone and everything.

When we are kind to people
or listen to them
or believe in them
or love them
or help them realize their deepest dreams
we help their spark grow bigger and brighter,
until their light shines out and fills up the world again,
one spark at a time.

And when it does, your own spark grows bigger
and shines brighter and brighter.

So the world is not broken, Grandpa?
The light is still there?

My grandfather smiled fondly at me.
Yes, Neh-shuma-leh.
The light is hidden, but the light is still there,
it will always be there,
and that changes everything.

This is the story of "The Birthday of the World,"
as it was given to me,
and now I give it to you.

It is not just my story;
it is your story, too.

One spark at a time,
we can change the world back to the way it was at the beginning—
whole and filled with light.

AUTHOR'S NOTE

Some stories are so timeless and true, they have been passed from hand to hand unchanged from generation to generation. "The Birthday of the World" is such a story.

My grandfather, a mystic and magnificent storyteller, told me the story of "The Birthday of the World" when I was four years old. This book is my retelling of his gift. Just as my grandfather gave it to me, I now give it to you.

Storytelling is one of the oldest and most powerful ways of making change. A good story gives us new ways of seeing and empowers us to change not only ourselves but the world around us.

I think that this story is a perfect story for our time. At this time in the history of things, it would be easy to be overwhelmed by despair and blinded by judgment, so paralyzed by fear that we feel powerless to make a difference. But we are all each enough, just as we are, to make a difference. You are enough, just as you are, to heal the world.

"The Birthday of the World" is about healing the world one heart at a time. It is about seeing with your heart. If you see with your heart, you can heal the world.

How do you see with your heart?

Seeing with the heart is not something that we are taught. It is a capacity that we are born with. It is something we remember. But sometimes we forget how to see with our hearts as we get older.

Like your eyes, your heart is an organ of vision, a way of seeing. When you look at everyone and everything with your heart, you see things that you would not see if you only looked with your eyes. It's like the difference between seeing things in black and white and seeing things in color. When you remember and begin to see with your heart again, the world fills with color. You see the light that is hidden in everyone and everything.

When you see with your heart, you notice things you have never noticed before. You can see below the surface of things, the appearances of things, and discover extraordinary things in ordinary people.

When you see with your heart, you see what is hidden; you see the beginnings of things: the seeds that will one day become a mighty forest.

When you see an acorn with your heart, you know that you are holding not a little woody thing but a great tree in the palm of your hand.

To see with the heart is to see the future.

I see the light in you, dear reader.
You are enough, just as you are, to heal the world.

Love, Dr. Rachel